Little Cloud

Parents' Magazine Press · New York

Little Cloud
by Robert Tallon

Library of Congress Cataloging in Publication Data

Tallon, Robert, 1939–
   Little Cloud.

   SUMMARY: A small cloud defies a mountain
and brings rain to a parched valley.
   [1. Clouds—Fiction.]   I. Title.
PZ7.T157Li   [E]   78-11061
ISBN 0-8193-0981-8
ISBN 0-8193-0982-6 lib. bdg.

For my father

"Little Cloud, where are you
going?" asked his friends.
"I want to see what's on the
other side of the mountain,"
he said, drifting past them.
"Come back," they called to him.
"You'll get lost."
But Little Cloud didn't listen.
He just floated away.

Soon he came to a very big
mountain. He looked at it
in wonder, for he had never
seen such a strange sight.
Suddenly, he heard an angry voice
shout, "Hey you! Watch where
you're going. You floated
right into my eye."
It was Mean Mountain, feared by
all living things for miles around.
"I'm sorry," said Little Cloud,
jumping back. "I just want to see
what's on the other side of you."
"Go away," yelled Mean Mountain.

"I won't go away," said Little Cloud.
Mean Mountain started to laugh,
loosening a few pebbles.
"You'll be sorry if you don't scram,
puff head!"

Little Cloud, not afraid, floated
around Mean Mountain and peeked
down at the valley below.
Everything was drying up.
The sad animals looked up at him.
Their only watering hole was
almost empty.

"Little Cloud, can you give us
some rain?" whispered a tall tree
with dry leaves.
"Every time rain clouds come by,
Mean Mountain scares them away."
"I'm too little," Little Cloud
replied, "but let me see what
I can do."

Then he floated up toward the
top of Mean Mountain, who, in a
rage, shouted, "I'll blast you
to the stars."
Little Cloud ignored him
and called down to his friends
in the valley.
"Don't worry. I'll be back.
I have a plan that I think will work."

Little Cloud glided away.
The sky was clear and there
was not another cloud in sight.
Just then an airplane flew by,
heading toward the sea.
He hopped on the tail.
In a little while, he became tired
and fell asleep.

When he woke up, he was floating
over the ocean. All around him
were his friends, fast asleep.
"Help! Wake Up!" he shouted.
"Shhh, Little Cloud, can't you see
we're taking our afternoon nap?"

"I'm sorry, but I have something important to tell you." He told them about Mean Mountain and about how he planned to save the valley. They agreed to help.

His plan was for each of them
to fill up with water over the ocean.
Then they would move together,
forming one big, powerful cloud.
They gathered in formation
and raced across the sky, with
Little Cloud in the lead. The sky
became dark as they came to
Mean Mountain and they stopped.

"Troublemaker," yelled Mean Mountain,
tossing rocks into the air.
Suddenly, a bolt of lightning
streaked out from Little Cloud.
It shot across the sky and
knocked off Mean Mountain's nose.
"My nose, my nose," he groaned.

Then the big cloud moved over the
valley, sprinkling rain all around.
It filled the watering hole.
It watered the grass and trees
and leaves. Everyone came out
to thank Little Cloud and
his brave little cloud friends.

Mean Mountain never said another
word again. He just kept looking
sadly at his broken nose
gathering dust on the ground.

Little Cloud stayed in the valley
and was happy. Even though
he grew bigger and bigger each year,
he was always called Little Cloud,
the hero of the valley.

About the author/illustrator

Robert Tallon, well-known for his many covers for *The New Yorker,* is the author/illustrator of such popular picture books as *Fish Story, Rhoda's Restaurant,* and *Zoophabets.* He has designed and written films for Sesame Street, and his paintings have been exhibited both in one-man and group shows at leading galleries and museums throughout the United States. Mr. Tallon lives in New York City.